What's Love

Got to Do With It?

Relationships 101

I0548147

Stories and Poems

by

Billie Hawkins

Copyright © 2012 Billie Hawkins

All rights reserved. No part of this book may be reproduced in any form or by any means, electronic or mechanical, including photocopying, recording, or by any information storage and retrieval system, without written permission from the author. This excludes a reviewer who may quote brief passages in a review.

ISBN: 978-0-9883374-0-4

Cover Design: Brittany J. Jackson

Published by G Publishing, LLC

Printed in the United States of America

CONTENTS

DEDICATION.. v

INTRODUCTION vii

JACQUE- A LOVE STORY 9

MATTIE JOHNSON AND HER MEN 16

POETRY IS.. 23

FIRST LOVE... 24

THE PLAYER.. 26

IT TAKES COURAGE TO LOVE 28

THE HANDYMAN.. 29

LOVE DON'T LIVE HERE ANYMORE 31

THE SNAKE 32

INTERNET BLUES.. 33

Introduction To The Poem- JEZEBEL............................. 35

JEZEBEL 36

STEP UP YOUR GAME 37

SMOOTH DADDY 38

ABUSE 39

THANK YOU, OPRAH 41

DEDICATION

This book is dedicated to my parents, especially my mom, Maude Stone, now deceased, who wrote and recited poetry all of her life and who passed her creative genes to me; to my wonderful husband, Robert Cecil Hawkins, also deceased, and the great love of my life; to my beautiful and loyal and loving daughters, Peggy Hawkins and Roberta Hawkins Harvey; to other relatives and friends who have always supported me in my creative endeavors, and to all the lovers everywhere.

INTRODUCTION

This book was written as a result of conversations with friends and acquaintances regarding their love relationships. It is also based on my own personal observations. The book is meant to entertain, to advise, and to inspire hope. Ultimately, what I hope the reader takes away from reading this book is that it takes courage to be vulnerable and fall in love and that "It is better to have loved and lost than never to have loved at all."

JACQUE- A LOVE STORY

He slipped into the seat beside her. She had been talking with one of her church members seated on her left. She turned, he smiled and their eyes met. There was an immediate attraction! He was handsome with beautiful gray hair that made him look very distinguished and he was impeccably dressed.

Julie had almost missed attending church this Sunday morning. She had turned off the alarm clock when it rang and decided to sleep fifteen more minutes. She awakened with a start to discover that she had only a little over an hour to shower, dress, and eat a bit before leaving for church to attend the eleven 0' clock service.

She vacillated- to go or not to go. Then she heard her mother's voice in her ear saying, "Julie, you go everywhere else, surely you can make it to church." Although her mother had been deceased for seven years, Julie listened.

As is customary, at the beginning of the service the minister asked everyone to shake hands and greet each other. When she shook his hand she felt a warm tingle go throughout her entire body. Had he felt it too? "Good morning, I'm Jacque." "Hi, I'm Julie."

The service began. The choir sang one of Julie's favorite hymns, "Precious Lord". When the song was over, someone sat down beside Jacque, causing him to move closer to Julie. During the reading of the announcements, he leaned over and whispered in her ear, "I'm so glad the lady sat beside me as that gave me an excuse to get closer to you." Julie thought, "Yes! He's actually flirting with me. Thank you, God!"

Julie had been looking for that special person ever since her husband had died. She had dated, but nothing serious. No one could "float her boat" as she used to say. She was at a loss to explain how giddy and how so much like a teenager she felt at that very moment.

As the choir began singing again, Jacque pulled a small pad from his pocket and asked her to write down her name, address and phone number as well as her email address. Her heart was pounding as she wrote down the information.

As they parted when the church service was over, Jacque told her that he was looking forward to getting together soon and that he would call her.

Driving home from church, Julie couldn't help thinking how glad she was that she had attended church that day, and how thankful to God she was that he had granted her prayer. She had been praying that someone special would come into her life and what better place to meet someone than in church.

Julie was ecstatic. She could hardly contain herself! As she pulled into her attached garage, she found herself singing, "At last, my love has come along."

The subject of the email was: To a lovely lady. It read: "Dear Julie, it was truly wonderful meeting you in church Sunday. Let's get together this weekend. I'll plan something and call you." It was from Jacque!

"A take charge guy—a guy who is true to his word. That's what I'm talking about!", thought Julie.

The call came on Thursday. "Hi Julie, this is Jacque. Let's get together Saturday. We'll see the Norman Rockwell exhibit at the Detroit Institute of Arts and have lunch. I'll pick you up at 12:00 noon."

They had a wonderful time at the D.I.A. viewing the many Norman Rockwell paintings that had graced the covers of The Saturday Evening Post for years. After viewing the exhibit, they had lunch in the D.I.A's cafeteria. As they ate, they talked about the exhibit and discovered that they were both graduates of Wayne State University. He had been married, had a family and was now divorced. She had been married had a family and was now widowed. They laughed, joked, talked about current events and lingered over lunch. He said she was pretty, she told him he was handsome.

They saw each other often after that first date. They held hands at the movies, went to plays, musicals and cultural events. They went to the taste fest and the ethnic festivals at Hart Plaza. They watched DVD'S at his home and hers. It was a wonderful Spring and Summer.

Julie was _so_ vulnerable, she was falling in love! They were both strongly physically attracted to each other. Jacque's kisses were mesmerizing! The sex was great! They couldn't get enough of each other!

In late August they went on a four day trip to the Shakespearean festival in Stratford, Ontario— their first trip together. It was wonderful! They saw five plays, Westside Story, Midsummer Night's Dream, Macbeth, Julius Caesar, and Julie's favorite, Cyrano De Bergerac, a story of unrequited love.

They did some sightseeing. Stratford is a lovely small town. They ate some delicious meals, shopped at the gift store and made mad passionate love! They returned to Detroit about noon on Sunday. Jacque took her home, carried in her luggage, said he had enjoyed the trip, gave her a big hug and a kiss and said he'd call her.

She waited for his call. Monday, Tuesday, Wednesday, Thursday, Friday—no call. This seemed a bit unusual, so Julie called him early Saturday morning to see what they were going to do during the weekend.

"Hello." "Hi Jacque, this is Julie." "Oh Hi, Julie. How are you?" His voice sounded strangely distant. "I'm calling you to see what you'd like to do this weekend." "I'm glad you called, Julie. I was going to send you an email." "An email about what?" "Well, I was going to tell you that I don't think we should date anymore". "What!" Julie felt a horrible feeling in the pit of her stomach. Did he say what she thought he said?

Then Jacque started telling her that he had become too attached to her, that he was beginning to care too much and that had not been in his plan. He went on to say that they should stop seeing each other and date other people. Julie was blindsided. She hadn't seen this coming. She knew he cared for her. She felt it. Why was he doing this?

After the initial shock and after regaining her composure she asked him if they could get together and discuss it further. He said that he had already made up his mind and that getting together would be a waste of time and that he wished her well.

Julie hung up the phone in a daze. She was devastated! She couldn't sleep, couldn't eat. She kept hoping he'd reconsider. She ran to the phone when it rang hoping it was Jacque- hoping he would have a change of heart. She missed him terribly!

As time passed and she did not hear from Jacque, her feelings ran the gamut from disbelief, to anger, to hope, and finally to the realization that this relationship was over. Kaput! Finished!

Had Jacque been telling her the truth? Had he really ever cared for her or had she been played? Whatever the case, Julie decided that her short relationship (6 months) with Jacque had been well worth it. He had made her so happy and she had beautiful memories. Their relationship had been full of fun, excitement and passion. It was great while it lasted and although it still hurts sometimes when she thinks of Jacque, she wishes him well. Julie has managed to move on and is now dating again and being the eternal optimist and a believer in the old saying, "It is better to have loved and lost than never to have loved at all," she is now looking for her next great love.

MATTIE JOHNSON AND HER MEN

My name is Mattie Johnson and I've got the blues. And do you know why I've got the blues? Because I love men, I mean I <u>love</u> me some men. But I just don't understand them.

For instance, I was walking down the street to the corner store. There were some raggedy looking men standing there on the corner. They all looked like they needed a bath and a shave.

When I got to the corner, one of them said, "Hey pretty momma, you sho lookin' good today!" Another said, "Hey, Miss Red, (I had on a red dress) don't you want to give me your phone number?" Now you know he was trippin' if he thought I was going to give him my phone number. If you want a queen like me, you have to act like a king.

I'm telling you, these men! You can't live with them, and you can't without them. Take for instance Bill. He was my first husband. Now Bill was a nice guy and a hard worker, but Bill had a poor sense of direction and was too proud to admit it. He'd drive miles out of the way before asking for directions. One day, we were going to

Billie Hawkins

a surprise birthday party for the wife of one of his co-workers. I asked if he had the directions written down and he said that he knew the way. We were supposed to be there no later than 4:45 so we all could hide in the kitchen to surprise the wife when she came home at 5:00 pm.

As Bill was driving, I looked at my watch and it was 4:30pm. I said, "Bill, are you sure you know where you're going? We should be there by now." Well, why did I say that. "Just sit back, and relax, I'll get us there. I don't need a co-pilot!" I could tell he was upset, so I just kept my mouth shut. Finally he said, "I guess I'd better stop at a gas station and ask for directions."

Neither of us had thought to bring our cell phones so he couldn't call his coworker. We finally came to a gas station and he went inside. I expected him to come out with directions written down but he had nothing in his hands. "Didn't you write down the directions?" "No," he said, "I've got them in my head."

Needless to say, we were extremely late for the party, arriving at 6:30 when the surprise was over.

I was so disgusted with that man because this wasn't the first time that this had happened. Why is it so hard for some men to ask for directions or to admit making a mistake? We argued constantly over this. Finally, I couldn't take it anymore and I divorced Bill.

John was my second husband. He was older than me, and was retired. I was still working. I liked John because he spoiled me. He enjoyed doing things around the house and he would fix my breakfast every morning and do any chores I asked him to do. He was kind and caring, and a real homebody.

When I'd come home from work, we would fix dinner together. After dinner he'd help with the dishes and then we'd watch TV or read in the den until bedtime. We had sort of gotten into a routine and I thought it was time for a change. Perhaps we could take a walk after dinner, or take a class together or invite a few friends in to play cards or go out to dinner or see a movie. One night, while watching TV, I decided to bring it up. I said, "Honey, it's time for a change." "What do you mean babe?" "I mean it's time for a change. Everyday we fix dinner, wash dishes and then sit here in the den on this same old couch watching this same old TV. It's time for a change." John said, "you know, I've been thinking the very same thing. It is time for a change."

I was so happy that John agreed with me! Now maybe we could spice things up a bit. John said, "Yeah honey, you are so right. We do need a change. I tell you what, this weekend we'll go over to Art Van furniture store and buy us a brand new couch and a brand new TV."

I couldn't believe my ears! He had missed the point altogether! Why is it that you just can't get through to some men?

Well, needless to say, despite all of John's good qualities, I had to let him go. Our relationship was just getting too <u>boring</u>.

And then, I met the love of my life! Frank Slithered into my life with his snake eyes and snake lies. He was smart, charming, handsome, never boring. He made me laugh and he treated me like a queen. We dated for about three months and then he asked me to marry him. I did. To tell you the truth, if he hadn't asked me to marry him, I would have asked him. He was everything I wanted. I was in love! He was husband number three.

We traveled, and went dancing. He was an excellent dancer. He called me every day at work to say he loved me and he sent flowers to me at work. Life was exciting and I was so happy! Then I found out he was a liar and a cheater!

This is what happened. Frank went out to the bar every Friday night with his buddies. That was fine with me; it gave me a chance to have some personal time for me. I would take a long bubble bath and give myself a manicure and a pedicure. I usually watched the 11:00 p.m. news and then went to bed, fully expecting that Frank would be sleeping beside me when I awakened the next morning. [I was a sound sleeper]

Well, when I awakened that Saturday morning about 7:00 a.m., there was no Frank! Frank hadn't come home. I was sick with worry, I began thinking that maybe he had been in an accident, or maybe he was somewhere hurt. I didn't know what to do. I didn't see his car in the driveway. I began to panic! Just as I was about to call one of his friends to see if he knew what had happened to Frank, I heard the key in the door. Frank came in, his usual charming self. I ran to him and gave him a big hug. "Where have you been? I was worried sick about you." "Hey babe, how's my best girl?", Frank said. "You'll never believe what

Billie Hawkins

happened. I left the bar when it closed and got into my car and the next thing I remember I woke up and it was morning. I had fallen asleep in the car."

I gave Frank another hug. It was then that I noticed the lipstick on his shirt and the hickey on his neck! I also smelled perfume and it wasn't my brand. I pushed him away. "You low-down, cheatin', poor excuse for a man! I thought you were with your buddies. Get out!" I wouldn't even listen to his explanation. I made him leave right then and only gave him time to pack a small bag.

Oh, he's called trying to get back with me and he even admitted that every Friday when I thought he was out with the guys he had been cheating on me. "Come on, babe, let me come home. You know I love you. She means nothing to me. It was just a fling." Oh, he was a real charmer alright. I still loved him and wanted to take him back, but I knew I could never trust him again, so we finally got divorced.

You know, despite all that men have put me through, I still <u>love</u> me some men. But I keep my guard up. Will there be a husband number four? Only time will tell, but I'll keep on trying until I get it right. Now, don't you go feeling sorry for me, because men are like buses. When one passes another one comes along, and I'm doing just fine, thank you. I take a bubble bath, give myself a manicure and pedicure, make sure my hair is fixed just right and I go out and have me some fun every Saturday night!

Billie Hawkins

POETRY IS...

Poetry is a beautiful sunrise.
Poetry is a lovely sunset.
Poetry is a baby's smile.
Poetry is a mother's love.
Poetry is a lover's caress.
Poetry is the way you move,
Laugh, kiss, make love.
Poetry is you.

FIRST LOVE

High school was great!
New friends, new freedom.

She liked her teachers.
Liked her classes,
Especially band.
That's where she first saw John.

He was <u>so</u> cute!
So popular—
Always surrounded by friends.
She liked him right away.

They both played in the band.
She got butterflies in her stomach
Whenever she was near him.
Such a crush!

John was tall and handsome,
Had a beautiful smile.
One day he smiled at her. Yes!
She smiled back.
He walked her to her bus,
Carried her books.

"Let's practice together after school", he said.

Billie Hawkins

They did.
Started dating on the weekends—
Movies, pizza, football games.

He kissed her.
She kissed him back.
It was sweet.
"I love you."
"I love you, too."
It was wonderful!
Then came the bad news.
"My father got transferred to New York,
we're moving Saturday."
She gasped!, "Oh no, John."
They cried.

So young—just sixteen.
Still, it hurt so much.
First love.

THE PLAYER

They met in March.
It was over by the end of Summer.

He sat beside her as the choir sang.
Tall and handsome.
The attraction was immediate.
Had he felt it too?

"Hi, I'm Jacque."
"I'm Julie."
He asked for her phone number.
Yes! God is good!

The call came the next day.
"Let's go to the art museum,
 There is a new exhibit on Saturday."
Wow! – Handsome and cultured.

They laughed, talked, held hands.
Movies, concerts, ethnic festivals,
Walks in the park, kisses.
Oh! The kisses!
Mad, passionate love!
Life was wonderful!

The phone rang. It was Jacque.

Billie Hawkins

"I'm becoming too fond of you,
And that was not in my plan.
I think we should stop seeing each other."

"What!" she was blindsided!
Where was this coming from?
"Can we talk about it?"
"No, I've made up my mind."

The tears fell. She was devastated!
Couldn't eat, couldn't sleep.
She thought he was her soul mate.
She called—he didn't answer.
Left messages- he didn't care.

She reconciled herself to the fact that
It was over—she had been "played".
Still, it hurt for the longest time.
But time heals all wounds.

And she's moved on.
She's seeing another guy,
Another lover, another soul mate,
Another "player?"

IT TAKES COURAGE TO LOVE

It takes courage to love,
To put one's self out there.
To be vulnerable.
To let go and let love.

To surrender to the bliss
Of a goodnight kiss.

To remember the pain
Of the loss of an old love
And yet, have the courage to love again.

THE HANDYMAN

My man is a handyman.
I found him in the yellow pages—
The handyman.

I needed someone to "fix" things—
A handyman.

The doorbell rang.
I opened it.
I couldn't believe my eyes!

Tall- skin like brown sugar.
Muscles rippling through his white t-shirt.
A tool belt hanging low on his waist.
I mean, the brother was fine!

"Hi, I'm George, the handyman."
That voice—so smooth, so deep.
What a turn on!

"You got some things that need fixin'?"
"Yes, I've got some loose doorknobs
And some of my windows are stuck tight with
paint.

"Can you start tomorrow?"

What's wrong with me? I don't understand.
Why am I flippin' out over this
Handyman.

He started coming three days a week
'Cause I kept finding things
That needed fixin'.

We had coffee and conversations.
We laughed, a lot.
He said I was pretty.
I told him he was hot!

It suddenly came to me with a start
The handyman was fixin' my broken heart!

I invited him to dinner
And we started going out.
And although it hadn't been in my plan,
You know what I did don't you ladies?
I made the handyman my man!

Billie Hawkins

<u>LOVE DON'T LIVE HERE ANYMORE</u>

Where did it go?
Darned if I know,
But love don't live here anymore.

I tried and I tried,
Even though you lied,
But love don't live here anymore.

You told me you'd be true
And that I could always count on you.
I've got to figure out what to do,
Cause love don't live here anymore.

THE SNAKE

He <u>slithered</u> into her life like a snake
And spread his venom.
She was mesmerized.
His wish was her command.

She couldn't eat,
Couldn't sleep.
Gave him all her time.
Gave him all her money.

He gave her great sex
And then, <u>slithered</u> away.

But you know what?
She'd take him back in a hot minute.

Some women never learn.

Billie Hawkins

INTERNET BLUES

You say she's just your friend,
Your buddy on the internet.
If she's just your friend
Then why turn off the computer
Whenever I walk in?

I can be your lover, your buddy
And your friend.
Besides, didn't we promise
To love each other until the end?

I'm just tryin' to help us
Keep our wedding vows.
So I'm giving notice,
Whoever tries to get in our way—
There's going to be <u>hell</u> to pay!

Now here's what you need to do
The next time she emails you—
Click on <u>delete</u>.
Better yet, click on <u>spam</u>.
<u>And</u> you need to <u>lose</u> her email address.

I just don't want you talkin'
To females on the internet,
Cause I <u>know</u> what can happen.

Don't you remember,
Or did you forget
That's the way <u>we</u> met.

Billie Hawkins

Introduction To The Poem- <u>JEZEBEL</u>

As a poet, I'm always looking for inspiration to write a poem and I was inspired to write this poem one Sunday at church.

The minister had asked all visitors to stand and introduce themselves. One of the members, a very vivacious young lady, introduced her visitor. She said, "I'd like to introduce my friend, whom I've just started dating. In fact, this is our first date."

Well, as a poet, my imagination got the better of me, and I wrote this poem. I call it <u>Jezebel</u>.

JEZEBEL

Look at me.
I'm one jazzy lady.
I'm one confident broad.

Now, I didn't get this way overnight.
I've been a work in progress.
You see, I didn't have much luck with men,
Until I decided to turn my <u>man</u> troubles
Over to the lord.

When men approach me now for a date
I say, "Let's make our first date a church date."
I invite them to the 11:00 service.
And we soon start attending church
On a regular basis.

Before they know what's happening,
They're hooked on me <u>and</u> the lord.

Folks around here
Have started calling me
A jezebel for Jesus!

Billie Hawkins

STEP UP YOUR GAME

I got caught up in your game,
And I only have myself to blame.

You wined and dined me,
Whispered sweet things in my ear,
Said you liked my smile—my style.

We talked for hours.
You said and did all the right things—
Made me feel like a queen.

Then you changed—
Started taking me for granted,
Didn't return my calls,
Canceled our dates.

I've been tolerating you for a while now,
And I need to tell you something.

Don't you <u>ever</u> get to thinkin'
That you're indispensable.
You need to know that you <u>can</u> be replaced.
And so, I'm going to put it to you like this,
If you want to keep this queen,
Either step up your game or, <u>step</u>!

SMOOTH DADDY

"Hey baby, you sure lookin' good!
Why don't you give me your phone number?
Daddy will take good care of you
Cause I sure know what to do."

"Standin' on the corner
Pants hangin' low.
No job, no money
Honey, you got to go."

"But baby, I got somethin' better than money,
I know how to float your boat.
I can make you feel <u>real</u> good honey."

"That won't pay the bills,
Buy the food
Or put clothes on my back.
And besides, I'm a queen.
And to get a queen
You have to act like a king.

So if I were you,
Here's what I'd do.
Get a job!"

Billie Hawkins

<u>**ABUSE**</u>

Love is not a black eye.
It hurt so bad!
Her eye began to swell.
"Where were you?"
"Why are you late?"

"I stopped by my sister's."
He hit her again—
Knocked her down.
Her head hit the floor.
There was blood.

"You're supposed to come
Straight home from work.
Next time, do as I say!"

This happens a lot.
He's a bully.
Why does she stay?
She says she <u>loves</u> him.
"I should have called.
It's all my fault.
I upset him."

"Oh, baby, I'm so sorry I hit you.
I didn't mean it.

You know I love you.
Please forgive me.
It won't happen again."

She's heard this before.
Still she can't leave.
What makes a woman
Let a man beat her
And then say, "It's all my fault?"

My sisters, it's not your fault.
You did nothing wrong.
And even if you did,
No man has the right to lay his hands on you!

Be brave, be smart.
Make a plan, then leave.
Leave while you still can.
Leave before you are a statistic.

He doesn't love you.
He doesn't love himself.
He won't stop. Leave!

Billie Hawkins

THANK YOU, OPRAH

If I'm not the one
Consider me gone.

I'm tired of your cheatin' ways,
You've been stepping out on me for days.

I've been takin' you back,
But this time, I'm givin' you <u>no</u> slack, jack.

You say, "I didn't mean it,
She means nothing to me.
She caught me at a weak moment,
She came on <u>so</u> strong
I just couldn't help myself.
You know I <u>love</u> you, babe.
Let your daddy come on back home."

These expressions of your affection
Are no longer workin' for you, chump!

You see, I been watchin' me some Oprah
And I been readin' me some books.
I been learnin' about self-esteem.
I been learnin' that I <u>am</u> somebody.

That's why I know

I'm too smart and too fine
To put up with your <u>stuff</u> anymore.

So leave! Get out!

I can find a man who treats me right
And one who's home when I wake up
In the middle of the night.

And one thing I know for sure
This sistah's gonna be alright.
So go! Put on that silly hat
And do whatever morons do,
But hear this—
I am <u>so</u> through with you!

Billie Hawkins

www.ingramcontent.com/pod-product-compliance
Lightning Source LLC
Chambersburg PA
CBHW031904170626
46807CB00004B/1894